DATE DUE

FROG LEGS

A PICTURE BOOK OF ACTION VERSE

BY GEORGE SHANNON

PICTURES BY AMIT TRYNAN

Greenwillow Books
An Imprint of HarperCollinsPublishers

CONTENTS

For Rafael Regan-Fong—G. S.   For Pauli—A. T.

Milar paper and acrylic paints were used for the full-color art. The text type is Kabel Medium.   Frog Legs: A Picture Book of Action Verse.
Text copyright © 2000 by George Shannon. Illustrations copyright © 2000 by Amit Trynan.   Printed in Singapore by Tien Wah Press.
All rights reserved.   http://harperchildrens.com
Library of Congress Cataloging-in-Publication Data: Shannon, George.   Frog legs: a picture book of action verse / by George Shannon ; pictures by
Amit Trynan.   p.   cm.   "Greenwillow Books."   Summary: Frogs enjoy such vigorous and joyful activities as stomping a sloppy plop step, flopping,
tipping, jumping, and doing the boogie buggaloo.   ISBN 0-688-17047-1.   [1. Frogs—Fiction.   2. Dance—Fiction.   3. Stories in rhyme.]   I. Trynan,
Amit, ill.   II. Title.   PZ8.3.S5285Fr   2000   [E]—dc21   99-12097   CIP
1 2 3 4 5 6 7 8 9 10   First Edition

Jumpabet 23

Sis-Boom-Ba 24

Trick or Treat 25

Just Like Me 26

Three-Legged Race

28

Balancing Act 29

Feet Feat 30

Ice 31

PUDDLE

Fresh puddle.
Tap. Mud'll
splash up high.
Jump. Double
stomp! Mud'll
plop into your eye!

JAMBOREE

Gather up the berries.
Spread 'em on the ground.
Step stomp klomp
as you circle round.

Add a pinch of sugar.
Tootsies everywhere.
Step stomp klomp.
Jam is in the air.

Spread it on a muffin
as you dance with glee.
Step stomp klomp.
It's a jamboree.

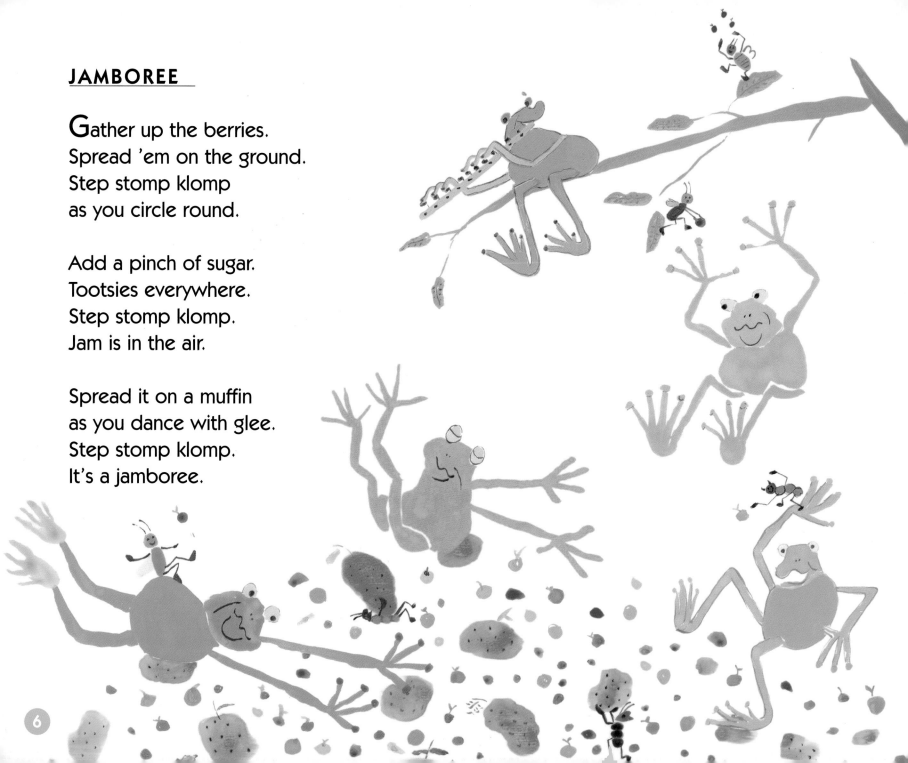

LIPS

Tulips in the garden.
Tulips in the park.
Tiptoe through the tulips
with your two lips in the dark.

Two lips in the garden.
Two lips in the park.
Four lips in the tulips
for some kissing in the dark.

7

SOCK RACE

Sock. Get set, go!
Hop. No stopping.
Lots of flopping.
Tipping, slipping.
Oops! Some flipping.
Falling. Crawling.
But no bawling.
Grinning. Winning
by a toe!

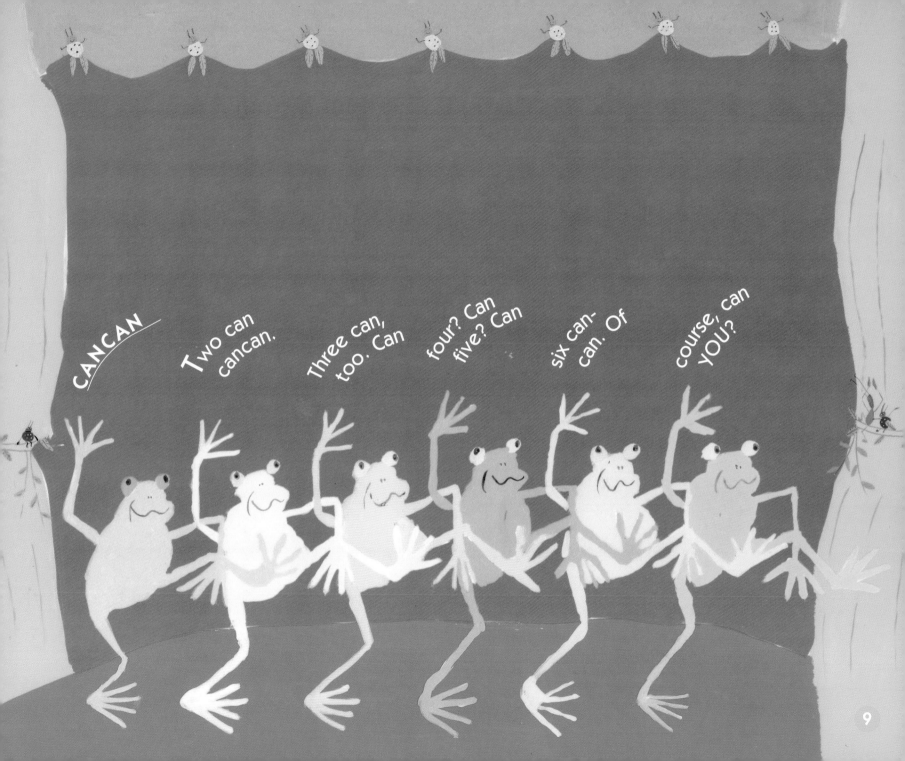

CANCAN Two can cancan. Three can, too. Can four? Can five? Can six cancan. Of course, can YOU?

FLAIR DANCE

Hand over hand, go round the ring.
Sharpen your shoulder blades, start to swing.
Jump back two, and tap your toes.
Walk the bridge of your partner's nose.

Do-si-do as you clap with flair.
Turn the key in a lock of your hair.
Slide to the left and jump with glee.
Tip the cap off your favorite knee.

Left by twos, turn right by ones.
Grab your nose before it runs.
That's the end. Go find a chair.
You know where, and I don't care!

HOPSCOTCH

You can wiggle.
You can prance.
You can waggle.
You can dance.
But with hopscotch
you gotta watch
and never touch the line.

You can quiver.
You can shake.
You can quaver.
You can quake.
And if you're watching
as you're scotching,
you'll land just fine.

Twinkle, twinkle, little star,
ballet dancer that you are.
Up on tippy-toes so high
like a swan about to fly.
Twinkle, twinkle, tiptoe star.
Twinkle-toes is what you are.

HOW TO PICK A PARTNER

No one to dance with? Fiddle-dee-dee.
Just snip a snapdragon or a chimp-pansy.

Tango through the treetops, or rumba with a roar.
Share a drink of water, then dance a little more.

If anyone laughs with a turned-up nose,
remember, you're lucky. No stepped-on toes.

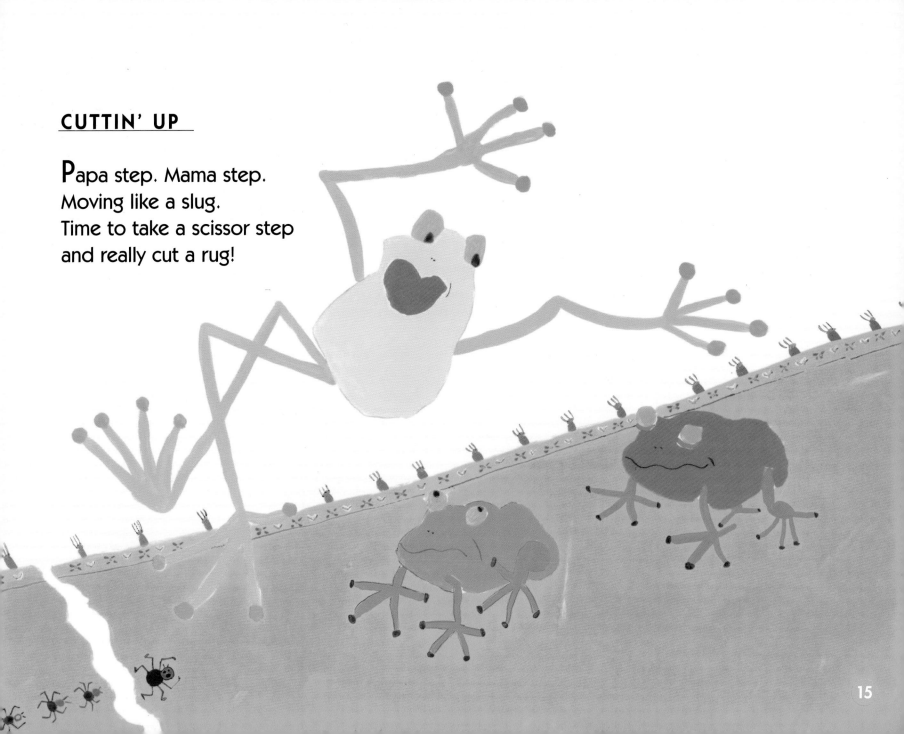

CUTTIN' UP

Papa step. Mama step.
Moving like a slug.
Time to take a scissor step
and really cut a rug!

HIGH DIVE

Head up. Arms out.
Take a breath and dive.
Double-flipping belly flop!
Score? Point five.

Tiptoes. Leap high.
Looping like a vine.
Twist a little. Side splash.
Five-point-nine.

Deep breath. Flip twist.
Show 'em how it's done.
Hands together. Quick splish!
You just won.

MUDDLE

Rainbow! Mud. Go
slimy slurping slow step,
ishy squishy goo step.
Tap a tiny splat step.
Muddy freckles fly.

Uh-oh. MUD. So?
Slide a slicker slip step.
Stomp a sloppy plop step.
Covered head-to-toe step.
Dance until you're dry!

JITTERBUG

Chigger bite.
Sitting tight.
Trying not to scratch.
Such an itch!
Just a twitch.
A little wiggle, too.

Chigger bite.
What a sight.
Twisting like a fool.
Flopping, flailing everywhere.
But scratch? I'll never do!

MAY POLE

Blue over
gold under
pink over
green under
blue over
gold and
around we go.

The longer the skipping,
the shorter the ribbon.
The shorter the ribbon,
the smaller the skip
till
bluegoldpinkgreen
it's all done!

BOOGIE BUGGALOO

We've got the toodle-noodle step for catching doodle bugs,
the later-gator step for catching tater bugs.
But when it comes to catching flies—
a sittin' step is the best.
We let a tongue do the rest.
But if it's not a fly,
it means we've got to try
another step or two of Boogie Buggaloo!

We've got the humble-stumble step for catching tumble bugs,
the bright 'n' fightin' step for catching lightnin' bugs.
But when it comes to catching flies—
a sittin' step is the best.
We let a tongue do the rest.
But if it's not a fly,
it means we've got to try
another step or two of Boogie Buggaloo!

TUTU, TOO

Here's a little dance with a hula hoop.
Wiggle, waggle, swing, and boop-oop-dee-doop.

Make it even better with a gold baton.
Wiggle, twirl, toss, and catch it with a yawn.

Better yet still, add a spinning plate.
Wiggle, twirl, spin, you're looking really great.

Blue ribbon best adds a tutu, too.
Wiggle, twirl, spin, toss down the avenue!

JUMPABET

A B C jump. D E F jump. G jump. H jump. I J K jump. L M N jump. O P Q jump. R S T jump.

U go out

as another comes in

jump.
2 feet. 3 feet.
4 feet. No feet.
Cross your 2 feet—
out the front
and in the back feet.

A B C jump . . .

23

SIS-BOOM-BA

Hop for the first step.

Second, bend low.

Third step, spring up.

Go, fool, go!

TRICK OR TREAT

Skip toe.
Tiptoe.
Going trick or treat.
Winds blow.
Step slow.
Sound of extra feet.
Owls, too.
BOO! Who?
Hearts all skip a beat.
Boo-hoo.
Time to
run a fast retreat!

JUST LIKE ME

One, two, three.
Make a line
behind the leader,
and the leader is me!

Be a worm and wriggle.
Be a bird and flap.
Be an egg and beat it
on the count of three.

One, two, three.
Make a line
behind the leader,
and the leader is me!

26

Be a moth and flutter.
Be a spider and spin.
Be a bee and buzz off
on the count of three.

One, two, three.
Make a line
behind the leader,
and the leader is me.

Be a fish and shimmy.
Be a whale and blow.
Be a splash, disappear
on the count of three.

One, two, THREE!

THREE-LEGGED RACE

Two together.
Count one.
Hop two.
Flop. Now,
try together.
Hop two,
three, four.
Slip, too.
Try another.
Hop up.
Two, three.
Flip, flop.
Trip into a
knot. Now,
all together,
hop to
get across
the line.

BALANCING ACT

Tight rope.
Slight rope.
Barely there to see.
First a wibble,
wobble step.
Then another three.

Left, right.
Step light.
Slowly turn around.
OOPS! Thank goodness,
the rope is on the ground.

29

FEET FEAT

Find a partner and grab a hand.
We're dancing to the music of the Rubber Band!

Jump right, shimmy, then twirl and clap.
We're dancing till we hear a gingersnap!

Cross step, shake it, and rock 'n' roll.
We're dancing till we see the salad bowl!

Slide left, holler, and start to swing.
We're dancing till we hear a diamond ring!

Back to the spot where you began.
We're dancing till we're sure the garbage can!

ICE

The moon is bright, the ice—just right,
for skating with some friends tonight.

Our first few steps—a shaky glide.
Then skid right! Sway back. Trip and slide.

No time for figure eights or arcs.
We're skating punctuation marks!

THE END